Let's Learn Aesop's Fables

The Ant and the Grasshopper

WINDMILL BOOKS

Published in 2018 by Windmill Books, an Imprint of Rosen Publishing | 29 East 21st Street, New York, NY 10010
Copyright © 2018 Windmill Books | All rights reserved. No part of this book may be reproduced in any form without permission in writing from the publisher, except by a reviewer. | Illustrator: Barbara Vagnozzi

CATALOGING-IN-PUBLICATION DATA
Title: The ant and the grasshopper.
Description: New York : Windmill Books, 2018. | Series: Let's learn Aesop's fables
Identifiers: ISBN 9781499483710 (pbk.) | ISBN 9781499483666 (library bound) | ISBN 9781499483567 (6 pack)
Subjects: LCSH: Fables. | Folklore.
Classification: LCC PZ8.2.A254 Ant 2018 | DDC 398.2--dc23

Manufactured in the United States of America
CPSIA Compliance Information: Batch BS17WM: For Further Information contact Rosen Publishing, New York, New York at 1-800-237-9932

It was a warm, sunny summer's day. There was a grasshopper in a field, and he was hopping around, chirping and singing very loudly.

Every day he sang, danced, played music, and ate to his heart's content.

3

After a morning of singing and dancing, the grasshopper started to feel tired. He lay back on a leaf, dozing in the sun.

On the ground, just beneath the sleeping grasshopper,
an ant was hard at work.

Huff!
Puff!

The ant's huffing and puffing woke up
the grasshopper, who looked down from his
comfy resting place to see what the noise was.

6

"Why are you **working** so hard? You should be resting and enjoying yourself, like me!" the grasshopper said to the ant.

"I have to work hard. I need to **store my food** and get my **nest ready** for **winter**," the ant replied.

"But winter isn't for months," the grasshopper said. "Come and play with me."

8

"I don't have time for playing," the ant said. "I have too much to do. You should start collecting food and preparing your home for winter."

"I don't want to work or be inside on a beautiful day like this!" replied the grasshopper.

9

So the grasshopper kept playing.
He sang songs and danced in the field.

Munch!
Munch!

He slept in the sun
and ate lots of food.

10

The ant continued to work,
storing food and making his nest
warm and cozy for winter.

In no time at all, the sun disappeared
and the weather turned cold.
The field became covered in a layer
of frosty white snow.

12

Winter had arrived!

Brrrr!

The ant was prepared for winter.
While the snowflakes fell outside,
the fire crackled inside his little nest.

Crackle!

He had enough food to see him
through the cold months ahead.

The grasshopper searched for food,
but he could not find any. He was very hungry.

He had no shelter from the falling snow and bitter winds.

The grasshopper remembered
the ant he had met in the summer.
He **knocked** on his door and asked
him if he had any **spare food**.

17

"Why don't you have any food of your own?"
asked the ant. "Did you not store any in the summer?
What were you doing?"

18

"I was so busy dancing
and singing and eating that
I didn't do any work at all!"
said the grasshopper.

19

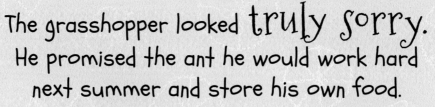

The grasshopper looked truly sorry.
He promised the ant he would work hard
next summer and store his own food.

So the ant gave him
as much food as
he could spare.

20

It was just enough to get the grasshopper through
the winter, but it was a miserable few months for him.

21

Next summer, the grasshopper was as good as his word.
He worked hard to store enough food for himself.

22

The grasshopper even found time
to help the ant, to make up for
his bad behavior and thank him.

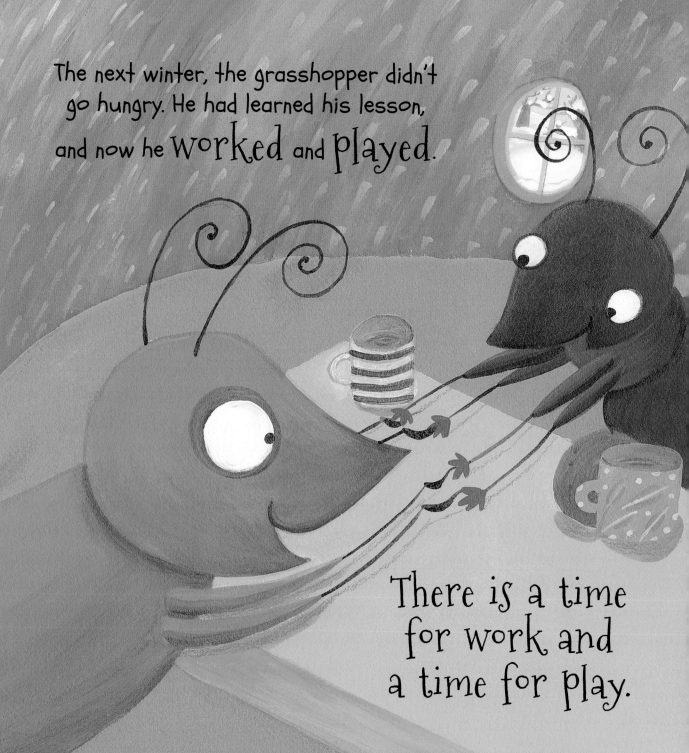

The next winter, the grasshopper didn't go hungry. He had learned his lesson, and now he worked and played.

There is a time for work and a time for play.